Thomas, Percy and the Squeak

**Based on *The Railway Series*
by The Rev. W. Awdry**

EGMONT

The engines on the Island of Sodor love the summer. Sometimes The Fat Controller holds concerts.

One day, the engines were very excited. Alicia Botti, the famous singer, was coming to Sodor to sing at The Fat Controller's concert.

"I'm bound to be chosen to collect her," boasted James. "I'm the brightest and the shiniest engine!" "Nonsense! I'm the most important!" huffed Gordon. Thomas wanted to feel important, too. "He might choose me," he said, hopefully.

Percy pulled up next to Gordon. His face was very grimy.

"Well, one thing's for sure," snorted Gordon, "He won't choose dirty Percy."

"I'm dirty because I work hard," said Percy proudly. And he wheeshed away.

The next day The Fat Controller came to decide which engine would collect the singer from the Docks. He didn't choose Gordon.

And he didn't choose James. He chose Thomas!

"Make sure Annie and Clarabel are squeaky clean," he said.

"Yes, sir!" said Thomas proudly.

He felt very important indeed.

Thomas hurried off to be cleaned. He parked next to Percy.

"Move aside," said Thomas. "I'm the important engine today."

"But I need a washdown!" wailed Percy. "My passengers will laugh at me."

"You'll have to wait," huffed Thomas. "Today I have to be squeaky clean."

"Then I'll have to go without being cleaned," said Percy, unhappily. "I'm a guaranteed connection!" He chuffed away, still very dirty.

Soon Thomas was shiny and squeaky clean.
He felt more important than ever. But as the
workers coupled Annie and Clarabel together,
they heard a strange noise. A funny sort of squeak.
"What's that?" asked Thomas, anxiously.
His Driver quickly oiled Annie and
Clarabel's undercarriage.
"That should take care of the annoying squeak,"
he said.

On the way to the Docks, Thomas heard the squeak again. He was worried. What could it be?

At the Docks, a big liner had brought lots of passengers to the Island of Sodor. Alicia Botti was waiting with The Fat Controller. Thomas squeaked into the quayside.

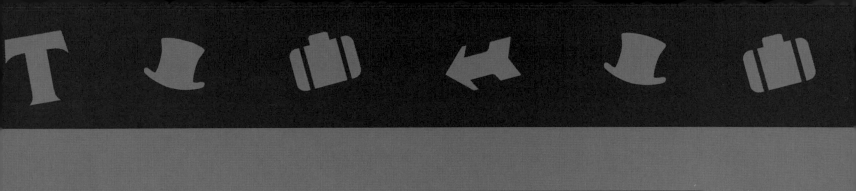

The Fat Controller held Clarabel's door open for the famous singer. He was pleased to see Thomas looking so clean and shiny. But as Alicia Botti was boarding the train, she saw a mouse inside the carriage!

"SQUEAK!" said the mouse.

"EEEEK! A mouse!" screamed Alicia Botti. And she screamed and screamed and screamed.

She screamed so loud and so long that windows broke all over town. Alicia Botti was very cross indeed.

"I can't possibly travel in coaches full of mice," she said.

The Fat Controller was very embarrassed. Thomas didn't feel important at all.

Just then, Percy returned from his guaranteed connection. He looked grimier than ever.

"Just look at the little green engine," Alicia Botti exclaimed. "So sweet . . . and dirty! Like a proper steam engine!"

The Fat Controller called Percy over at once.

The Fat Controller and Alicia Botti boarded one of Percy's carriages and sat down.

Percy puffed out of the station as proudly as can be.

When they arrived at the concert, Alicia Botti thanked Percy for such a comfy ride.

The Fat Controller was very pleased with Percy.

"You are a Really Useful Engine!" he said.

Later that day, Thomas was waiting at the washdown when Percy chuffed up beside him. "I'm sorry I was so cheeky," said Thomas. "You go first."
"Thanks, Thomas. It's good to be friends again," said Percy. "But where is your mouse?"
"You'll see!" grinned Thomas.

The Fat Controller had made the mouse her very
own home in the corner of Tidmouth sheds.
And Thomas named her Alicia.

First published in Great Britain 2002
by Egmont UK Limited
239 Kensington High Street, London W8 6SA
This edition published 2007

Thomas the Tank Engine & Friends™

A BRITT ALLCROFT COMPANY PRODUCTION
Based on The Railway Series by The Reverend W Awdry
© 2007 Gullane (Thomas) LLC. A HIT Entertainment Company

ISBN 978 1 4052 2974 6
ISBN 1 4052 2974 8
1 3 5 7 9 10 8 6 4 2
Printed in China